For Ben and Frankie,
paddling on the other side
of the globe. S.

A TEMPLAR BOOK

First published in the UK in 2019 by Templar Books,
an imprint of Bonnier Books UK,
The Plaza, 535 King's Road, London, SW10 0SZ
www.templarco.co.uk
www.bonnierpublishing.com

Text and illustration copyright © 2019 by Sebastien Braun
Design copyright © 2019 by Templar Books
10 9 8 7 6 5 4 3 2 1

ISBN 978-1-78741-515-7

This book was typeset in Providence Sans
The illustrations were created digitally

Publisher: Lisa Edwards
Edited by Katie Haworth
Designed by Genevieve Webster
Production controller: Sian Cheung

Printed in Latvia

templar
books

Raj
and the
BEST HOLIDAY
EVER!

The Perfect Holiday

PLANNING : SECRETS REVEALED

HOW TO ORGANISE YOUR LIFE

MANAGING EXPECTATIONS

ATLAS 2019

The World

TRAVELLING With Children

Seb Braun

Dad and I are going on holiday today.
I know it's going to be the
BEST HOLIDAY EVER!

Dad is getting everything ready.
There is SO MUCH to put
in the car!

Are we going
to America?

"Not that far, Raj," says Dad. "We're going camping."

I am **very** excited. I've read lots of camping books, so I tell Dad all about it.

You also need hiking boots to climb big mountains!
R4J1
And best of all, you can go in a canoe!
You know a lot more about this than me, Raj!
R4J1

After a while, Dad stops at a petrol station. I need to stop too!

PIT STOP

I don't know how Dad knows where to go, but he does.

Team Bear

And after a **really long** time . . .

. . . We arrive at the campsite. It's beautiful!

"Look Raj, the tents look like fairy lights," says Dad.
"This is going to be the best holiday EVER!"
I say back.

R4J1

He says there is space for
our little tent beside a
HUMONGOUS one.

Dad asks me to hold the torch so he can see.

He **really** knows how to put up a tent!

Inside the humongous tent next door
there is a family of bears. They ask Dad
if he needs any help . . .

What if we all pitch in, buddy?

But Dad says, "No thank you."
He's doing such a good job that he doesn't!

When we get inside the tent to go to sleep, I realise that I need the toilet. I tell Dad but he doesn't say anything, so I tell him again.

Dad, I really, really, really, REALLY need to go!

I tell him until he gets up to take me there.

It's dark, and on the way Dad trips over something. I ask a very important question.

When we wake up in the morning, I am **very** excited.
Dad says it's too early to be so excited,
but I don't agree.

We're going to cook **breakfast** on our
camp stove!

Grumble . . .
puff . . . hurumph . . .
Wet matches . . .

But things don't go quite the way Dad planned.

The family of bears asks Dad if we want to join them,
but Dad says, "No thank you."

We eat cornflakes instead.

After breakfast Dad says, "Let's go on our **big walk!**"

So we do!

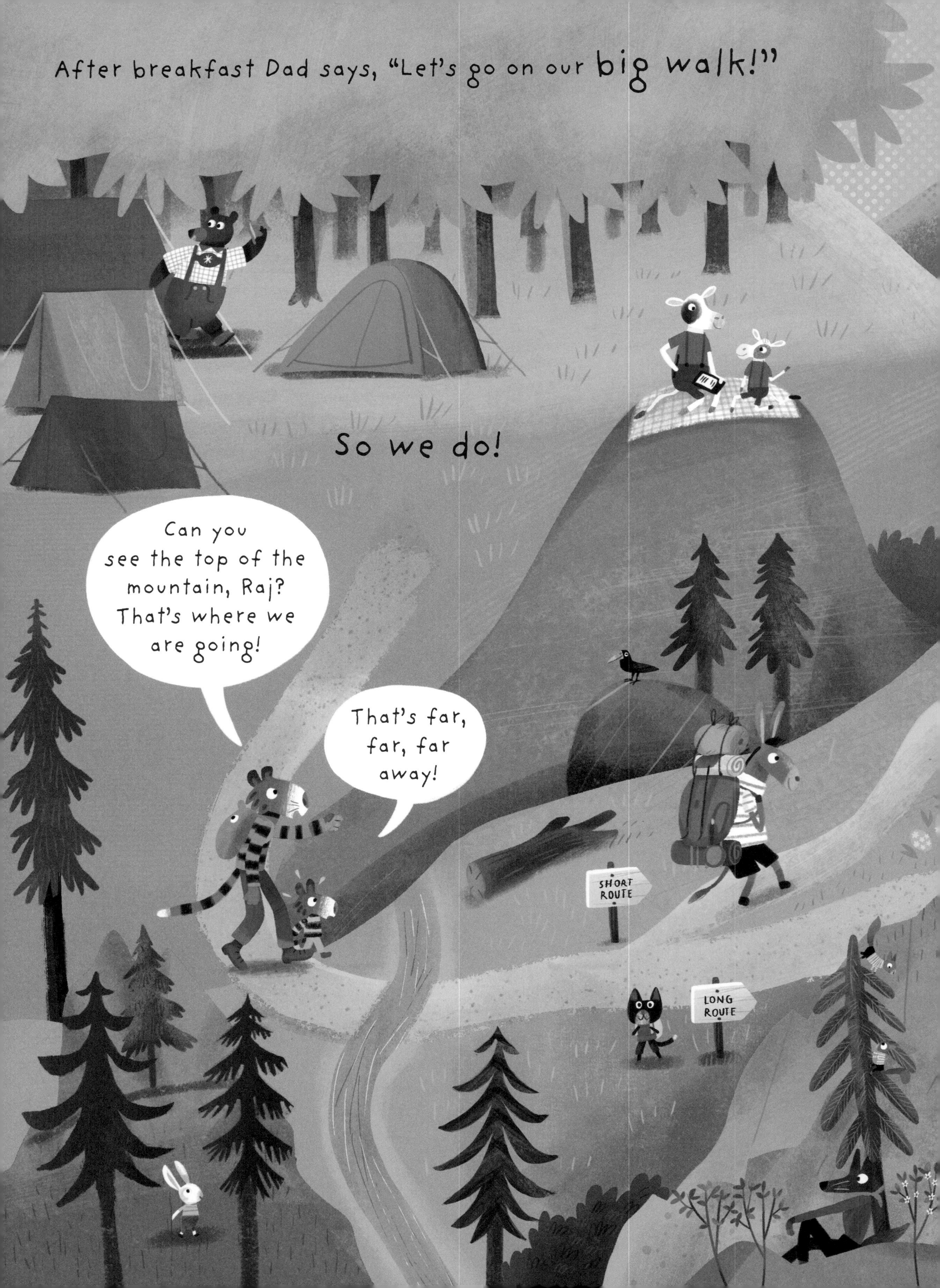

There is **so much** to see!

We walk for ages, but we make it to the top!

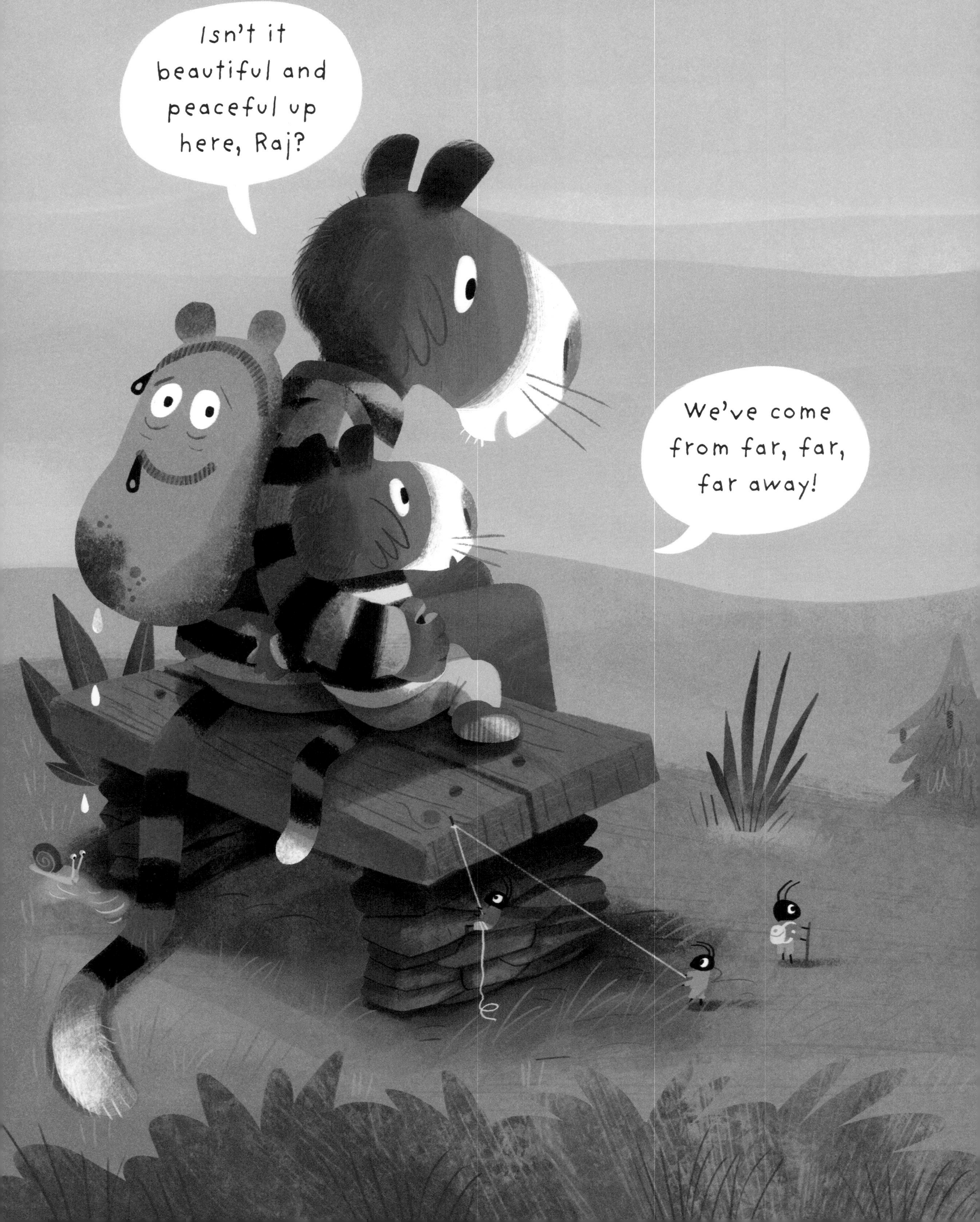

But just then . . .

🎵 SHE'LL BE COMING ROUND THE MOUNTAIN WHEN SHE COMES . . . 🎵

The bears ask if we want to come with them
and take the short cut . . .

But Dad says, "No thank you," and we go back
the way we came.

Walking down the mountain takes a **long, long** time.
I am **so tired.**

Dad says it isn't far, but it seems like it is.

Soon, I am really thirsty so Dad takes out the bottle . . .

There is no water left in our bottle.

I feel really sad.
"This is the
WORST HOLIDAY EVER!"
I tell Dad.

"We're nearly back at camp," says Dad.
"And after lunch I have a special surprise."

It's a BRILLIANT surprise!

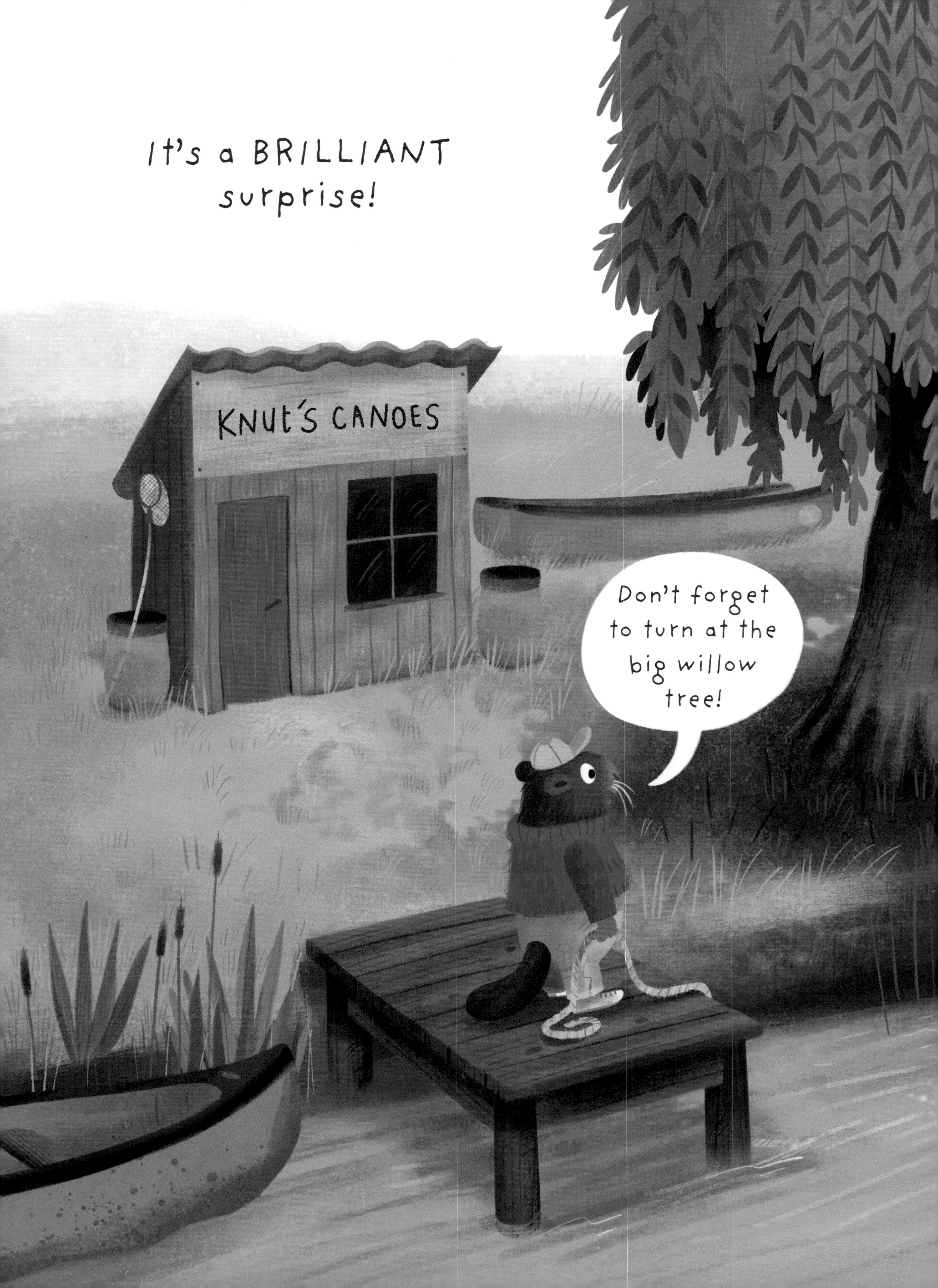

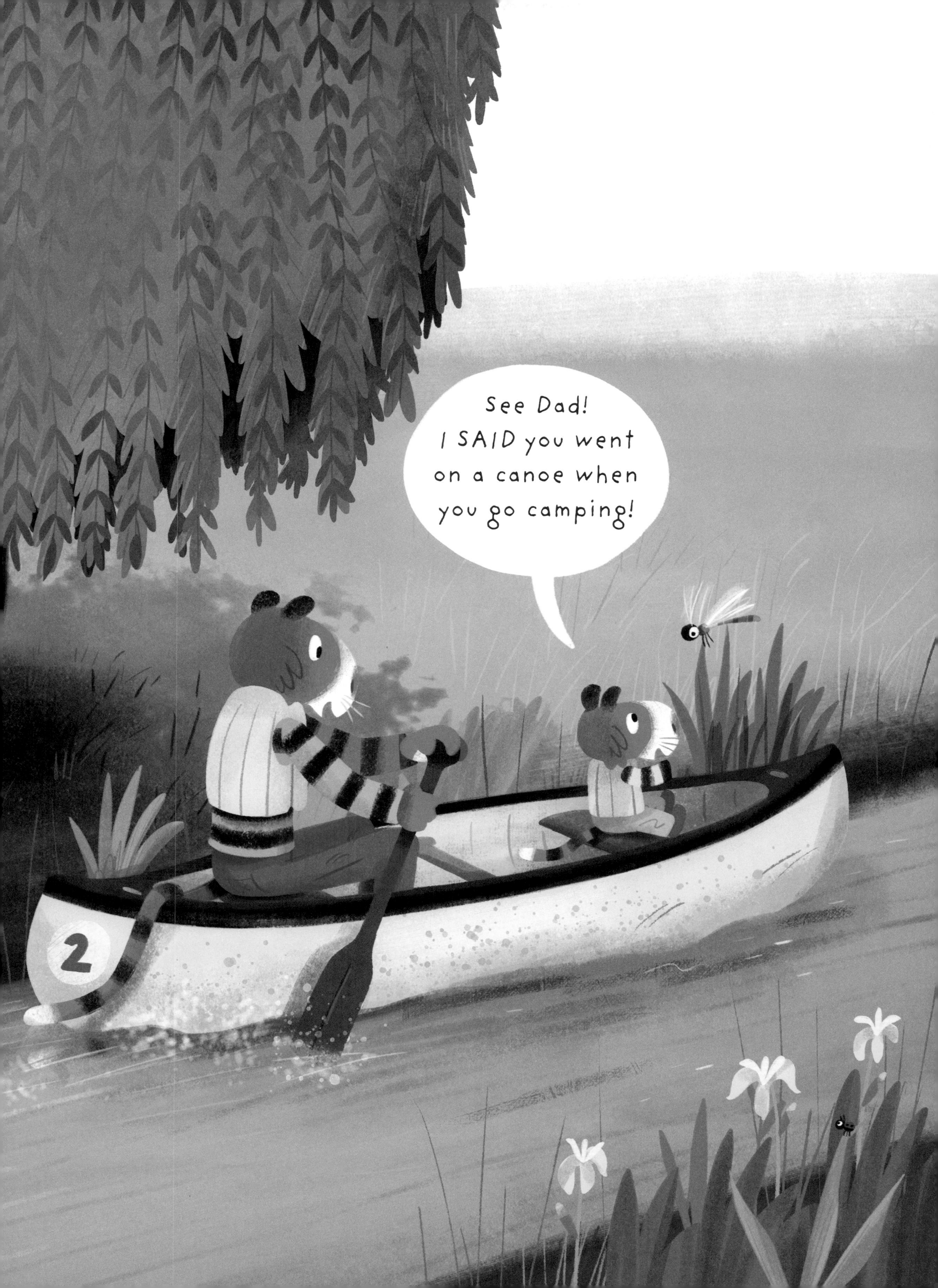
See Dad! I SAID you went on a canoe when you go camping!

I tell Dad that I know just the song for a surprise like this, and we sing it.

Dad is enjoying singing so much that he closes his eyes.

He doesn't see something quite important.

And then our **paddle is lost!** Dad doesn't know what to do.

We are going down the river **fast** and there is lots of white foamy water ahead. I am feeling **scared.**

Just then, me and Dad see the family of bears.

The mummy and daddy bear ask Dad if he needs help.

This time Dad says, **"YES, thank you!"**

The bear family . . .

does something . . .

AMAZING!

And we are saved.
Just like that!

Then the Littlest Bear
asks us a question.

Do you want to come to our campfire singalong tonight?

And I say,
"YES, THANK YOU!"

We have so much fun that I ask Dad
if we can do this again next year.

He says yes.

And then I tell him something else . . .

"This is
DEFINITELY the
BEST HOLIDAY
EVER!"

The end!

More picture books from Templar:

ISBN: 978-1-78741-234-7

ISBN: 978-1-78741-386-3

ISBN: 978-1-78741-411-2

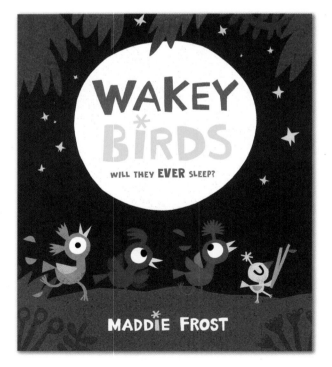

ISBN: 978-1-78741-366-5